WALT DISNEY'S
The Three Little Pigs

ILLUSTRATIONS BY THE WALT DISNEY STUDIO

ADAPTED BY MILT BANTA AND AL DEMPSTER

from the Walt Disney Motion Picture "The Three Little Pigs"

GOLDEN PRESS
Western Publishing Company, Inc.
Racine, Wisconsin

This Little Golden Book was produced under the supervision of

THE WALT DISNEY STUDIO

Walt Disney Books

Little Golden Books here bring you, in gay color, delightful stories and illustrations adapted from the world-famous Walt Disney Motion Pictures. In them you will find *Pinocchio, The Three Little Pigs, Bambi, Dumbo, Cinderella, Peter Pan,* as well as many other well-loved Disney characters.

Thirty-Seventh Printing, 1973

ONCE UPON A TIME there were three little pigs who went out into the big world to build their homes and seek their fortunes.

The first little pig did not like to work at all. He quickly built himself a house of straw.

Then off he danced down the road, to see how his brothers were getting along.

The second little pig was building himself a house, too. He did not like to work any better than his brother, so he had decided to build a quick and easy house of sticks.

Soon it was finished, too. It was not a very strong little house, but at least the work was done. Now the second little pig was free to do what he liked.

What he liked to do was to play his fiddle and dance. So while the first little pig tooted his flute, the second little pig sawed away on his fiddle, dancing as he played.

And as he danced he sang:

"I built my house of sticks,
I built my house of twigs.
With a hey diddle-diddle
I play on my fiddle,
And dance all kinds of jigs."

Then off danced the two little pigs down the road together to see how their brother was getting along.

The third little pig was a sober little pig. He was building a house, too, but he was building his of bricks. He did not mind hard work, and he wanted a stout little, strong little house, for he knew that in the woods near by there lived a big bad wolf who liked nothing better than to catch little pigs and eat them up!

So slap, slosh, slap! Away he worked, laying bricks and smoothing mortar between them.

"Ha ha ha!" laughed the first little pig, when he saw his brother hard at work.

"Ho ho ho!" laughed the second little pig. "Come down and play with us!" he called.

But the busy little pig did not pause. Slap, slosh, slap! went bricks on mortar as he called down to them:

"I build my house of stones.
I build my house of bricks.
I have no chance
To sing and dance,
For work and play don't mix."

"Ho ho ho! Ha ha ha!" laughed the two lazy little pigs, dancing along to the tune of the fiddle and the flute.

"You can laugh and dance and sing," their busy brother called after them, "but I'll be safe and you'll be sorry when the wolf comes to the door!"

"Ha ha ha! Ho ho ho!" laughed the two little
pigs again, and they disappeared into the woods
singing a merry tune:

"Who's afraid of the big bad wolf,
The big bad wolf, the big bad wolf?
Who's afraid of the big bad wolf?
Tra la la la la-a-a-a!"

Just as the first pig reached his door, out of the woods popped the big bad wolf!

The little pig squealed with fright and slammed the door.

"Little pig, little pig, let me come in!" cried the wolf.

"Not by the hair of my chinny-chin-chin!" said the little pig.

"Then I'll huff and I'll puff and I'll blow your house in!" roared the wolf.

And he did. He blew the little straw house all to pieces!

Away raced the little pig to his brother's house of sticks. No sooner was he in the door, when Knock, knock, knock! There was the big bad wolf!

But of course, the little pigs would not let him come in.

"I'll fool those little pigs," said the big bad
wolf to himself. He left the little pig's house.
And he hid behind a big tree.

Soon the door opened and the two little pigs
peeked out. There was no wolf in sight.

"Ha ha ha! Ho ho ho!" laughed the two little
pigs. "We fooled him."

Then they danced around the room, singing
gaily: *"Who's afraid of the big bad wolf,*
                The big bad wolf, the big bad wolf?
                Who's afraid of the big bad wolf?
                Tra la la la la-a-a-a!"

Soon there came another knock at the door. It was the big bad wolf again, but he had covered himself with a sheepskin, and was curled up in a big basket, looking like a little lamb.

"Who's there?" called the second little pig.

"I'm a poor little sheep, with no place to sleep. Please open the door and let me in," said the big bad wolf in a sweet little voice.

The little pig peeked through a crack of the door, and he could see the wolf's big black paws and sharp fangs.

"Not by the hair of my chinny-chin-chin!"

"You can't fool us with that sheepskin!" said
the second little pig.

"Then I'll huff, and I'll puff, and I'll blow your house in!" cried the angry old wolf.

So he huffed

and he PUFFED

and he *puffed*

and he HUFFED,

and he blew the little twig house all to pieces!

Away raced the two little pigs, straight to the third little pig's house of bricks.

"Don't worry," said the third little pig to his two frightened little brothers. "You are safe here." Soon they were all singing gaily.

This made the big bad wolf perfectly furious!

"Now by the hair of my chinny-chin-chin!" he

roared, "I'll huff, and I'll puff, and I'll blow your
house in!"

So the big bad wolf huffed and he PUFFED,
    and he *puffed* and he HUFFED,
but he could not blow down that little house of
bricks! How could he get in? At last he thought
of the chimney!

So up he climbed, quietly. Then with a snarl,
down he jumped—right into a kettle of boiling
water!

With a yelp of pain he sprang straight up the chimney again, and raced away into the woods. The three little pigs never saw him again, and spent their time in the strong little brick house singing and dancing merrily.